About the author

Thomas Hardy was born in 1840,
and died in 1928.

He wrote about the West Country
and the lives of those who lived there.

About the story

Before television or films,
people had other forms of entertainment
especially in the country.

The most popular were dances, or 'Reels'.
Everybody, young or old,
went to them.
The music for the reels was played on the
violin or 'fiddle'.

THOMAS HARDY'S

he Fiddler
)f the Reels

Peter Leigh

blished in association with The Basic Skills Agency

Hodder & Stoughton

A MEMBER OF THE HODDER HEADLINE GROUP

Acknowledgements
Cover: Lee Stinton
Illustrations: Jim Eldridge
Photograph: Hulton Getty

Every effort has been made to trace copyright holders of material reproduced in this book. Any rights not acknowledged will be acknowledged in subsequent printings if notice is given to the publisher.

Orders; please contact Bookpoint Ltd, 39 Milton Park, Abingdon, Oxon OX14 4TD. Telephone: (44) 01235 400414, Fax: (44) 01235 400454. Lines are open from 9.00–6.00, Monday to Saturday, with a 24 hour message answering service.
Email address: orders@bookpoint.co.uk

British Library Cataloguing in Publication Data
A catalogue record for this title is available from the British Library

ISBN 0 340 77461 4

First published 2000
Impression number 10 9 8 7 6 5 4 3 2 1
Year   2005 2004 2003 2002 2001 2000

Typeset by GreenGate Publishing Services, Tonbridge, Kent.
Printed in Great Britain for Hodder and Stoughton Educational, a division of Hodder Headline Plc, 338 Euston Road, London NW1 3BH, by Redwood Books, Trowbridge, Wilts

I

Mop Ollamoor was a musician.
He played the violin.

He played so sweetly and so sadly,
it could have drawn an ache
from the heart of a gate-post.

He was called Mop
because of his long, greasy black hair.
He perfumed it
and arranged it in curls round his face.

Mop could make any child
burst into tears in a few minutes.
All he had to do was play
one of the old dance tunes.

But it was on young women
that Mop had most effect –
especially sensitive and emotional women.

Such a young woman was Caroline Aspent.
Caroline was a pretty, soft-mouthed girl.
She already had one young lover,
but Mop Ollamoor's heart-stealing melodies
deeply touched her.

One evening, as she was going home,
she paused on the bridge near his house
to rest.

Mop was standing on his door-step, as usual,
spinning music through his fingers.
He laughed as the tears rolled down
the cheeks of the little children
hanging around him.

Caroline leaned lazily over the wall.
She pretended to watch
the stream under the bridge.
But Mop knew she was really listening to
him.

Soon her heart was aching with wild desires.
She wanted to dance,
to lose herself in a dance
that went on forever.

She tried to shake off her fascination.
She needed to go on, to get away.
But that meant she had to pass him.

She stepped forward.
As she drew closer,
she found her steps
keeping time with the music.
Now she was nearly dancing along.

She looked up at him.
She saw that he was smiling at her,
laughing at her roused feelings.

She couldn't stop her feet from dancing
until she was a long way past his house.
Nor could she shake off
the strange infatuation for hours.

After that day, whenever there was a dance
where Mop Ollamoor was playing,
Caroline was there.

infatuation – a very strong desire, an obsession.

Mop's power over her grew.
She would be sitting quietly at home,
when she would suddenly start
from her seat.
It was like getting a shock.
Then she would burst into tears.
It would take half an hour
for her to grow calm again.

No-one knew what was wrong,
but if you had been listening very closely
you would have heard a man's footsteps
outside.

It was Mop Ollamoor,
as the girl well knew;
but he was not coming to her
but to another who lived further on.
Only once did it happen
that Caroline could not control herself.
She cried out,
'O – O – O – !
He's going to her, and not coming to me!'

To do Mop justice,
he had not at first thought often of Caroline,
or spoken much to her.
But as soon as he found out her secret,
he could not resist a little playing
with her over sensitive heart.

The two met,
and grew to know each other well,
though only in secret.

II

The only other person who knew
Caroline's secret was Ned, her first lover.
He wanted to marry Caroline,
but knew it was hopeless.
Her feelings for Mop
were growing stronger and stronger.

Finally Ned put the question to her flatly,
would she marry him,
then and there, now or never?

Caroline said 'No!' but very sadly.
She liked Ned, and so did her family.
But Ned could not play the violin.
He could not draw your soul out of your body,
like a spider's thread,
withy wind – a
country breeze
till you felt as limp as a withy wind.
In fact Ned had no ear for music,
and could not sing two notes in tune,
much less play them.

The No from Caroline
gave Ned a new start in life.
He decided to move away from her
and went to London.

In London he found regular work.
For the next few years
he was never out of a job.
He never spoke about Caroline.
In his quiet lodging
he did his own cooking and
looked after himself.
Gradually he shaped himself
to the life of a bachelor.

Four silent years passed.
Then Ned received a letter from Caroline.
The writing was uncertain,
as if written with a trembling hand.
She told him of the trouble
she had gone to find his address.
And then she spoke
of why she had written.

'Four years ago I was so foolish
as to refuse you.
My stubbornness
has been a grief to me many times since,
especially recently.
As for Mop Ollamoor,
he has been gone nearly as long as you, Ned.
Where he is I do not know.
I would gladly marry you now, Ned,
if you were to ask me again.
I would be a tender wife to you till my life's
end.'

A tide of warmth surged through Ned
as he read this.
This was from his Caroline,
who had been dead to him these many years.
Now she was alive to him again.
Ned did not show his feelings much.
Now, after his first surprise,
the letter stirred him deeply.

Ned doesn't do
things on impulse.

Ned was a steady and cautious man.
He did not answer the letter that day,
nor the next, nor the next.
He was having a good think about things.

When he did answer it,
there was a great deal of common sense
mixed in with tenderness.
But that tenderness itself
was enough to show that he still cared.
The hold she once had over him
was still there.

He said –
'It's all very well for you
to have a change of heart now.
Why wouldn't you have me
when I wanted you?
I expect you have learned
that I'm not married.
But suppose my feelings
are fixed on another?
You ought to say you are sorry.

Still, I'm not the man to forget you.
But seeing how I've been used,
and what I have suffered,
you can't just expect me
to come to you.
But if you come to me,
and say you are sorry, as is only fair,
why, yes, I will marry you.
I know what a good woman
you are at heart.'

Caroline said in her reply –
'How good it is of you, Ned,
to treat me so well,
after my hot-and-cold treatment of you.
I'll take up your offer with all my heart.
I'm not looking forward to the journey,
because I have never been on a train before.
I will come to you,
and tell you how sorry I am.
I will say I am sorry.
I shall try to be a good wife always,
and make up for lost time.'

And so it was agreed.
They would meet at the station,
and the day after, Ned said
he would marry her.

Remember at this time distances seemed much further. Roads were very bad, and the railway had only just been invented.

III

And so one early afternoon,
Ned came from his work.
He hurried towards the station to meet
Caroline.
It was wet and chilly,
but as he waited on the platform
in the drizzle he glowed inside.
He had something to live for again.

In those early days of railways
the passengers sat in open trucks.
There was no protection whatever
from the wind and rain.
So when the train pulled into the station,
they were wet, blue with the cold,
sneezing and chilled to the marrow.

marrow – bone

In the bustle and crush
of everybody getting off,
Ned soon saw the slim little figure
he was looking for.
She came up to him with a frightened smile –
still pretty, though damp, weather-beaten,
and shivering from the wind.

'O Ned!' she spluttered, 'I – I – '
He clasped her in his arms and kissed her.
She burst into floods of tears.

'You are wet, my poor dear!
I hope you'll not get cold,' he said.
He looked her over.
As he looked down,
he saw she was holding the hand of a child –
a little girl of three or so.
Her little face was wet and blue.

'Who is this – somebody you know?' Ned
asked.

'Yes, Ned. She's mine.'

'Yours?'

'Yes – my own.'

'Your own child?'

'Yes!'

'But who's the father?'

'The young man I had after you courted me.'

'Well – as God's in –'

'Ned, I didn't say it in my letter, because,
you see, it would have been so hard to explain!
I thought that when we met
I could tell you face to face
how she happened to be born.
I hope you'll excuse it this once, dear Ned,
and not scold me.
I've come so many, many miles!'

'This means Mr Mop Ollamoor, I reckon!'
said Ned, his face pale.

Caroline cried,
'But he's been gone away for years!
I'd never had a young man before!
And I was so unlucky to be caught out
the first time he took advantage of me.
Some of the girls down there
go on like anything!'

Ned stood in silence, thinking.

'You'll forgive me, dear Ned?'
she added, beginning to cry.
'I've been honest with you after all.
You can pack us back again,
if you want to –
though it's hundreds of miles,
and so wet, and night coming on,
and I with no money!'

'What the devil can I do!' groaned Ned.

There was no sadder sight
than this pair of helpless creatures.

They stood on the platform in the drizzle,
with the pretty clothes
in which they had set out from the country
all muddy and wet.
There was weariness on their faces,
and fear of him in their eyes.
For the child began to look
as if she thought she too
had done some wrong,
and the tears began to roll
down her chubby cheeks.

little maid – a country name for a little girl

'What's the matter, my little maid?' said Ned.

'I do want to go home!' she cried unhappily,
and my toes be cold,
and I shan't have no bread and butter no
more!'

'I don't know what to say to it all!' said Ned.
He turned and walked a few steps
with his head down.
Then he turned, and looked back at the little
girl.

'Want some bread and butter, do you?'

'Ye-e-s!'

'Well, I dare say I can get you a bit!
Naturally, you must be hungry.
And you, too, for that matter, Caroline.'

'I do feel a little hungry.
But I can keep it off,' she murmured.

'Folk shouldn't do that,' he said gruffly …
'There, come along!'
He caught up the child, and added,
'You must stay here to-night, anyhow, I
suppose!
What else can you do?
I'll get you some tea and supper.
As for this business,
I'm sure I don't know what to say!
This is the way out.'

They went their way, without speaking,
to where Ned lived,
which was not far off.

There he dried them and made them
comfortable.
He made some tea,
and they sat down thankfully.
The room seemed cosier
with this ready-made family.
Ned looked fatherly
as he sat with them.
Presently he turned to the child
and gave her a kiss.
Then he looked sadly at Caroline,
and kissed her also.

'I don't see how I can send you back all them
miles,' he growled, 'now you've come
all this way just to join me.
But you must trust me, Caroline,
and show you've real faith in me.
Well, do you feel better now, my little maid?'

The child's face lit up.
Her mouth was busy with
the bread and butter.

'I did trust you, Ned, in coming,
and I shall always!'

And so, without saying anything definite,
he quietly accepted the fate
that Heaven had sent him.

The next day they were married,
and began to settle down.
Ned found that Caroline
made a very good wife and companion.

As time passed,
there was less and less work in London,
and finally Ned found himself with none.

They were both country born and bred,
and longed to go back.
And so they decided to leave London,
and that Ned should look
for work near home.
His wife and her daughter would stay with
Caroline's father
until he found a job
and a home of their own.

IV

She thinks the country people will be impressed with her big city ways.

despised – looked down on (because she was an unmarried mother)

As she journeyed down to home
Caroline felt tinglings of pride.
She had left there two or three years before,
in silence and under a cloud.
Now she was returning,
a smiling London wife with London ways
to where she had once been despised.

The train did not stop at their village,
but at a town a few miles away.
Ned decided to stay there for a bit,
and ask around for a job.
Caroline and her little girl
would walk on towards their village,
and Ned would catch them up halfway
at an inn.

It was a pleasant evening,
and it was a joy for Caroline
to walk back the well-remembered way.
By the time they got to the inn,
the moon was up, and they were tired.

Caroline opened the door.
Almost straight away
a man she remembered by sight
came forward with a glass in his hand.
'Surely,' he said,
'it's little Caroline Aspent?
Come in and have a drink.'

Caroline did not exactly want this,
but since it was offered, she agreed.
'Come and sit down,' he said.
The centre of the room was empty,
and all the chairs were round the edges.
When Caroline had found an empty one,
and sat down with her little girl,
she saw why.
It was a dance.
Over in the other corner stood Mop,
rosining his bow
and looking just the same as ever.

rosin – a special ointment on the bow of a violin to make it sound more.

She didn't think he would recognise her,
or have any idea who the little girl was.
And she was pleased to find
she could face him quite calmly.
Her time in London had given her
control over herself.
Mop Ollamoor no longer
had any effect on her.

Then the dance began,
and things changed for Caroline.

She felt a tremor inside her,
and her hand started to shake.
She could hardly set down her glass.
It was not the dance nor the dancers,
but the notes of that old violin
which thrilled her.

After all these years
they still had the same witchery,
the same power over her.
How it all came back!
There was the same figure against the wall,
the large, oily, mop-like head of him.
And beneath the mop the face
with closed eyes.

Perhaps it was the drink
but his cunning playing
and the old familiar tunes
were having the same effect on her as ever.
She wanted to laugh and cry
at the same time.

A man whose partner
had dropped out of the dance,
stretched out his hand.
He asked her to take his partner's place.
She did not want to dance and
tried to show it.
But it was no good.
Tired as she was
she grasped her little girl by the hand,
and plunged into the dance,
whirling about with the rest.

The others were all local.
Gradually they recognised her.
She danced on and on,
wishing that Mop would stop.
His playing was causing her feet to ache.

At last the dance ended,
and she was offered another drink.
She took it,
feeling very weak
and overcome with emotion.

Several people left.
Caroline was going to as well,
when Mop began another tune.
He must have recognised her
because it was the tune
she could least resist.
It was the tune he had played
when he had first seen her
leaning over the bridge.
In despair Caroline began to dance again.

The tune went on and on,
full of sadness and sweetness.
It was a kind of blissful torture.
Round and round danced Caroline.
The room began to swim.
One by one the others dropped out
exhausted.
Caroline was left alone in the room
with the little girl and Mop.

Mop looked at her
as if for the first time.
He smiled his dreamy smile.
He threw everything he could into the tune –
every expression, every bit of feeling.
It would draw tears from a statue.

Round and round drifted Caroline helplessly.
The child began to cry.
'Stop, mother, stop,' she whimpered,
as she held on to her hand,
'Let's go home!'

Suddenly Caroline sank to the floor,
and lay still.
She had fainted.

Mop stopped playing instantly,
and went to the little girl
who was bent over her mother.

V

The other dancers came back in.
They had heard something unusual.
They immediately tried to revive Caroline
by fanning her and opening the windows.

At that moment Ned arrived at the inn.
When he went in,
he found Caroline in hysterics,
weeping violently.
She could not speak.

'What has happened?' cried Ned.

They told him about the dance and the
fiddler.

'What fiddler?'

He was one who used to be known
in those parts,
but hadn't been seen recently.
He had just turned up tonight.

'His name? What is his name?'

'Ollamoor! Mop Ollamoor!'

If I swing for it – if I
hang for it

'Blast him!' cried Ned. 'I'll beat
his skull in for him,
if I swing for it tomorrow!
Where is he? And where –'
he swung round the room,
'where – where's my little girl?'

But Mop Ollamoor had disappeared,
and so had the child.

25

He rushed outside
with everyone following.
It was dark.
On one side of the inn was a wood,
on the other a moor.

Ned dashed off one way with some men,
while others went off the other.
After about twenty minutes
they had all returned.
There was no Mop and no child.

Ned sat down, his head in his hands …

The others whispered,
'Well – what a fool the man is,
and has been all these years,
if he thinks the child is his.
Everybody knows otherwise!'

'No, I don't think she's mine!'
cried Ned hoarsely,
as he looked up from his hands.
'But she is mine, all the same!
Haven't I nursed her?
Haven't I fed her and teached her?
Haven't I played with her?
O, little Carry – gone with that rogue – gone!'

'You haven't lost your misuss, anyhow,'
they said to cheer him up.
She's been sick.
'She's throwed up the drink,
and she is feeling better,
and she's more to you
than a child that isn't yours.'

'She isn't!
She's not so special to me,
especially now she's lost the little girl!
But Carry's the whole world to me!'

26

'Well, like as not you'll find her tomorrow.'

'Ah - but shall I?
Yet he can't hurt her - surely he can't.
Well - how's Caroline now?
I am ready. Is the cart here?'

They had sent for a cart
to take Caroline the rest of the way.
Sadly the two went on home.

Next day she was calmer,
but her will seemed shattered.
She seemed very little worried for the child
though Ned was nearly driven wild
by his love for a child not his own.

Everyone expected
Mop to return the child after a day or two.
But time went on,
and neither he nor she were heard of.

Ned thought that maybe
Mop had the same musical power over her
as he had over Caroline herself.

Weeks passed,
and still they had no clue
as to where the fiddler or the girl were.

Then Ned took a sudden hatred
towards his home.
Then he heard a rumour through the police.
A man resembling Mop and a child
had been seen at a fair near London.
He was playing a violin and
she was dancing on stilts.

Ned set off immediately for London,
with Caroline in tow.
He did not find the child,
but from then on
he spent his time searching the streets for her.
He would start up in the night, saying,
'That Mop's torturing her to keep him in
money!'

To which his wife would answer,
'Don't disturb yourself so, Ned!
You're stopping me sleep!
He won't hurt her!' and fell asleep again.

People thought that maybe
Mop and the child had gone to America.
Perhaps she was keeping him
with her dancing.
Either way, neither of them were ever seen
in that area again.